A Note to Parents and Caregivers:

Read-it! Readers are for children who are just starting on the amazing road to reading. These beautiful books support both the acquisition of reading skills and the love of books.

The RED LEVEL presents familiar topics using common words and repeating sentence patterns.

The BLUE LEVEL presents new ideas using a larger vocabulary and varied sentence structure.

The YELLOW LEVEL presents more challenging ideas, a broad vocabulary, and wide variety in sentence structure.

The GREEN LEVEL presents more complex ideas, an extended vocabulary range, and expanded language structures.

When sharing a book with your child, read in short stretches, pausing often to talk about the pictures. Have your child turn the pages and point to the pictures and familiar words. And be sure to reread favorite stories or parts of stories.

There is no right or wrong way to share books with children. Find time to read with your child, and pass on the legacy of literacy.

Adria F. Klein, Ph.D.
Professor Emeritus
California State University
San Bernardino, California

Editor: Bob Temple
Creative Director: Terri Foley
Editorial Adviser: Andrea Cascardi
Copy Editor: Laurie Kahn
Designer: Melissa Voda
Page production: The Design Lab
The illustrations in this book were rendered digitally.

Picture Window Books
5115 Excelsior Boulevard
Suite 232
Minneapolis, MN 55416
1-877-845-8392
www.picturewindowbooks.com

Printed in the United States of America.

Library of Congress Cataloging-in-Publication Data
White, Mark, 1971–
The wolf in sheep's clothing : a retelling of Aesop's fable / written by Mark White ;
illustrated by Sara Rojo.
p. cm. — (Read-it! readers fairy tales)
Summary: Retells how the wolf's plan to get into the sheep pen backfires when
the farmer butchers him for a lamb dinner.
ISBN 1-4048-0220-7
[1. Folklore. 2. Fables.] I. Aesop. II. Rojo, Sara, 1973– ill. III. Title. IV. Series.
PZ8.2.W55Wo 2004
398.2—dc21   2003006304

Read-it! Readers
Yellow Level

The Wolf in Sheep's Clothing

A Retelling of Aesop's Fable

Written by Mark White

Illustrated by Sara Rojo

Library Adviser:
Kathy Baxter, M.A.
Former Coordinator of Children's Services
Anoka County (Minnesota) Library

Reading Advisers:
Adria F. Klein, Ph.D.
Professor Emeritus, California State University
San Bernardino, California

Susan Kesselring, M.A.
Literacy Educator
Rosemount-Apple Valley-Eagan (Minnesota) School District

Picture Window Books
Minneapolis, Minnesota

There was once a clever wolf.

Each night, he watched the farmer
lock his flock of sheep
behind a tall fence.

The fence was too high
for the wolf to jump over.

"How can I get inside the fence?"
the wolf asked himself.

One day, the wolf had an idea.
He would dress up as a sheep!

That night, the farmer
brought the sheep home.
The wolf slipped into the flock.

"Come on," the farmer said. "In you go."

The farmer didn't notice anything strange
as the wolf walked past him into the pen.

15

Click! The farmer locked the gate.

At last, the wolf was
on the other side
of the fence!

The wolf tried to decide.
which sheep to eat first.

Just then, the farmer came back.

"I need something for my dinner,"
the farmer said.

He entered the gate and killed a sheep.

Soon, he discovered the sheep
he had killed was actually a wolf!

The farmer said to himself,
"It is dangerous to pretend to be
something you are not."